Prissy &Pop
Deck the Halls

For Penelope, my piggie angel who fostered my love for pigs,
and for Marlent and Kristy, who helped bring Prissy and Pop into the world

Special thanks to P and P Designs for Prissy's precious bows and to Grafton Studios.

Prissy and Pop Deck the Halls
Text copyright © 2016 by Melissa Nicholson
Illustrations copyright © 2016 by HarperCollins Publishers

ISBN 978-0-06-243996-3

Typography by Chelsea C. Donaldson
16 17 18 19 20   SCP   10 9 8 7 6 5 4 3 2 1
First Edition

Prissy&Pop
Deck the Halls

By Melissa Nicholson
Photographs by Petra Terova

HARPER
An Imprint of HarperCollinsPublishers

**"Wake up, Pop!"** Prissy calls. "Rise

and shine!"

"But I'm so warm and cozy," says Pop.

"Silly Pop, it's three days until Christmas, and there's

still so much to do!" says Prissy.

And two little piggies begin their holiday tasks.

"You know what we should do first?" says Pop.

"Trim the tree," says Prissy.

❄ ❄ ❄

"Oops," Pop says. "We made a mess."

"Santa won't care," says Prissy.

Pop hopes that's true.

"I can't wait until Santa comes!" squeals Pop.

"Let's make cookies for Santa next!" says Prissy.

Two little piggies make cookie dough . . . and they

only eat a *little* bit of it!

Soon the cookies are cut into holiday shapes.

"I'll do the icing," says Prissy.

"I'll do the sprinkles!" says Pop.

Prissy and Pop bake the cookies until they're

nice and crunchy.

"Santa will love these," says Prissy.

"Oh no, we forgot to mail a Christmas card to Santa!" Prissy squeals.

"Quick, let's send one with the directions to our house so Santa doesn't get lost," says Pop.

Two little piggies hope Santa gets the card in time. Hooves crossed!

Happy Holidays! Love, Prissy & Pop

The next day Prissy remembers the gingerbread-

   house kit.

The piggies get to work decorating the little house.

"It looks just like our house!" says Pop.

"Do you think a tiny gingerbread Santa will visit it?"

   asks Prissy.

"Ho ho ho!" Pop laughs.

"This house needs some winter cheer," says Prissy.

With only one day before Christmas Eve, she gets to work. Snip snip snip!

Soon there are paper snowflakes all over the house.

"It's a winter wonderland!" cries Prissy.

The piggies take a break with some holiday punch.

Ah! Refreshing.

Prissy thinks about gingerbread Santa. Then she thinks about piggie Santa.

What if our Christmas card to Santa got lost in the mail? Prissy wonders. *How will he know where we live?*

How will he eat the cookies we made for him?

She decides not to say this out loud.

She doesn't want to worry Pop.

"Time to make popcorn for our Christmas movie!"

   says Pop.

Pop pops the popcorn—his favorite part!

"You're a good popcorn popper, Pop!" says Prissy.

   "Mmm, smells delicious!"

Two little piggies sit down and watch *How the*

   Hog Stole Christmas.

It's finally Christmas Eve!

Prissy and Pop warm up their voices for carols.

"La la la la la," they sing. "Jingle bells, jingle bells,

jingle all the way . . ."

Two little piggies sing in perfect piggie harmony.

Their Christmas jobs are almost done, and soon

it's time to go to sleep. Just a few more

Christmas Eve activities.

Prissy and Pop change into their piggie pajamas.

They put out cookies for Santa.

And they hang their little piggie stockings.

I hope I hope I hope Santa comes this year, Pop thinks.

Prissy's Christmas would be ruined if he didn't!

Please please please, Santa, don't get lost, Prissy

thinks. *Pop's Christmas would be no fun without you.*

Prissy and Pop try hard to stay awake.

But they're so sleepy, and the fire is so warm. . . .

Soon two little piggies fall fast asleep.

Finally it's Christmas morning! Prissy and Pop open their eyes.

"Oh my piggie goodness!" says Pop. "Santa came to our house after all!"

"Oh good piggie golly!" says Prissy. "He didn't get lost! I mean, not that I was worried."

"Of course not," says Pop. "Me neither. Not for a second."

Santa brought the little piggies a whole pile of presents.

Board games, clothing, treats, and books—

everything a pair of piggies could ever want!

"Merry Christmas," they both say.

"I'm glad Santa came," says Prissy.

"Me, too," says Pop. "But—"

"But," says Prissy.

"The best part of Christmas is you!" two little piggies

say together.

Priscilla & Poppleton's Holiday Favorites

prissy loves:

- making snowflakes
- singing carols
- writing a letter to Santa
- watching Christmas movies
- dressing in her holiday best
- being with Pop

pop loves:

- hanging up stockings
- snuggling in Christmas pj's
- popping popcorn
- eating Christmas cookies
- lending a hoof to animals in need
- being with Prissy